PASSPORT TO
MEXICO

Carmen Irizarry

Franklin Watts

London/New York/Sydney/Toronto

Copyright © 1987 Franklin Watts Limited

First published in Great Britain by
Franklin Watts Limited
12a Golden Square
London W1R 4BA

First published in the USA by
Franklin Watts Inc.
387 Park Avenue South
New York
N.Y. 10016

First published in Australia by
Franklin Watts Australia
14 Mars Road
Lane Cove
NSW 2066

UK ISBN: 0 86313 440 8
US ISBN: 0-531-10271-8
Library of Congress Catalog Card No: 86-50571

Editor: Lynne Williams
Design: Edward Kinsey
Illustrations: Hayward Art Group
Consultant: Keith Lye

Photographs: Tony and Marion Morrison,
ZEFA, Tony Hutchings, Mexicolore, Bridgeman
Art Library, BBC Hulton Picture Library, NASA

Front cover: Tony and Marion Morrison, ZEFA
Back cover: Tony and Marion Morrison

Phototypeset by Keyspools Limited
Color reproduction by Hongkong Graphic Arts
Printed in Belgium

Contents

Introduction

Mexico occupies a unique position between the continents of America. It forms the southernmost part of North America, and has strong historical and economic links with the United States. The people and culture of Mexico, however, have greater ties with the countries of Latin America. Thus the country bridges two vast and very different civilizations.

Mexico is a fascinating blend of Indian and Spanish cultures. This mixture is reflected in Mexican life-styles, customs and beliefs and ancient traditions. Mexico is, however, changing fast. Its people are eager for economic and social progress. The country is now a place of great contrasts, where new industry and high technology are eclipsing many of the old ways.

In just a few decades, Mexico has been transformed from a relatively poor country to a far more prosperous and industrialized nation ready to play a prominent role in the affairs of the world.

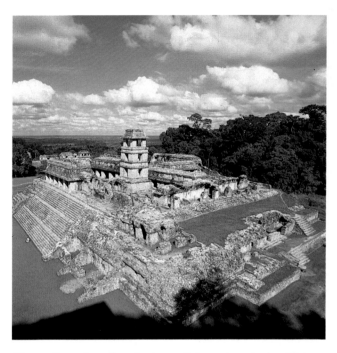

Above: Remains of ancient Indian civilizations are found in many parts of Mexico. This is a Mayan Temple at Palenque.

Below: A main road into Mexico City. Expressways and high-rise buildings are very typical of the new Mexico.

The land

Mexico is a long, narrow country bordered by the Pacific Ocean to the west, and the Gulf of Mexico and the Caribbean Sea to the east. Extending down the west coast is a long peninsula known as Baja California. In the southern region another great landmass – the Yucatán Peninsula – thrusts far into the Gulf of Mexico.

The country's landscape is extremely varied. It includes deserts, grasslands, snow-capped mountains and humid tropical forests. In the north, where the land is arid or semi-arid, temperatures can range from very hot to bitter cold. The southern coastlands, in contrast, have a sub-tropical or tropical climate and lush vegetation. In the south, too, there is a rainy season, between May and October.

The Pacific coastal plains are very arid in the north and give way to tropical, humid conditions in the south. The Yucatán and the Gulf Coast form the largest lowland area in Mexico. Its northern parts are dry while others are covered by swamps and lagoons.

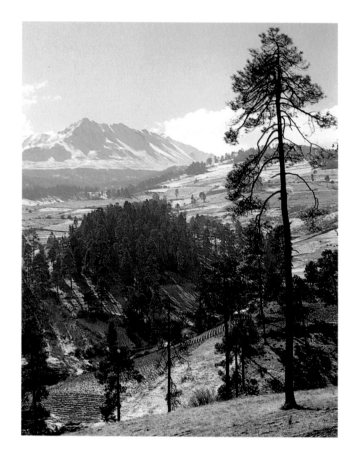

Above: Pine forests cover the slopes of the Sierra Madre Occidental mountain range, near Toluca, in central Mexico.

Left: Oaxaca in southern Mexico lies at an altitude of 1,500 m (4,921 ft) above sea level. It is not easy for farmers to grow crops in this arid land.

Left: Acapulco, on the Pacific coast, has a humid tropical climate.

Below: Tropical plants, such as bananas, grow in profusion along river valleys,as here in Jalisco State.

Altitude, however, is the dominant physical feature in Mexico. Beginning south of Mexico City, and running north like the arms of a letter Y, are two great mountain chains – the Sierra Madre Occidental and the Sierra Madre Oriental. Among their peaks are Orizaba (Citlatépetl), the country's highest point, and the famous Popacatépetl, whose Indian name means "Smoking Mountain". Both are dormant volcanoes over 5,000 m (16,500 ft) high. The Southern Highlands, or Sierra Madre del Sur, extend from Mexico City along the Pacific coast.

The largest and most important feature of Mexico is, however, the Central Plateau which extends from the United States border to south of Mexico City. It rises to altitudes between 1,000 and 2,000 m (3,300 and 6,600 ft). The Plateau covers over half of Mexico and contains most of the major cities. Its fertile land and equable climate are able provide much of Mexico's food requirements.

The people

Modern Mexico is the product of two very different civilizations – the American Indian and the Spanish. These two cultures have blended to form a unique Mexican way of life.

The first settlers in what is now Mexico were Indian peoples who crossed into North America from Asia several thousand years BC. In time they formed into many distinct tribes and built great civilizations. The Mayas left exquisite sculptures, temples and made many scientific discoveries. Other Indian empires also flourished, including the Toltec, Zapotec and Mixtec.

When the Spanish first arrived in Mexico in 1519, the most powerful tribe were the Aztecs. They were quickly defeated by the Spanish and from 1522 to 1821, Mexico was a colony of Spain and called *New Spain*. Over the centuries the Spaniards and Indian peoples intermarried. Today nearly 80 per cent of the Mexican population are of mixed ancestry or *Mestizos*.

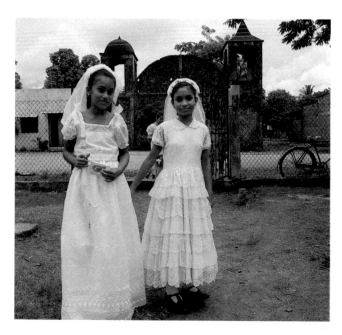

Above: Girls about to take their First Communion. The Catholic faith plays a very important part in Mexican life.

Below: Any crowd of people will illustrate the mixture of Indian and Spanish races that form the Mexican population.

Mexico City is the country's most important industrial base. Served by efficient road, rail and air links, it has a huge concentration of industries, including oil refining, textiles and clothing manufacture, and food processing. Half of the electricity generated in Mexico is used by these industries, which also employ 60 per cent of the city's total workforce. Tourism is also one of the major contributors to the city's economy.

In education and culture, Mexico City is equally important. The world-famous Palace of Fine Arts and the Museum of Anthropology are located here. The city also has nearly a quarter of Mexico's schools, as well as a vast university.

The rapid growth of its population is the city's greatest social problem, for there is much overcrowding. The city also suffers greatly from air pollution. The surrounding mountains unfortunately help to trap the fumes from factories and cars.

Above: Mexico City sprawls over a vast area. In the foreground is the splendid Palace of Fine Arts.

Below: A disastrous earthquake in 1985 brought down many buildings in the city, causing great loss of life.

Fact file: land and population

Key facts

Location: Mexico lies roughly between latitudes 33° and 15° North, and straddles the Tropic of Cancer. It is the third largest country in Latin America, and is bounded by the US to the north and by Guatemala and Belize to the south.

Main parts: Mexico is divided into 31 states, and one federal district, Mexico City, Mexico includes two large peninsulas: Baja California in the northwest (1,220 km/758 miles long); and in the south, the Yucatán Peninsula.

Area: 1,972,547 sq km (761,605 sq miles).

Population 76,800,000 (1984 estimate).

Capital: Mexico City

Major cities with 1980 census populations except Mexico City:
Mexico City (18,000,000) – 1984 estimate
Guadalajara (2,245,000)
Monterrey (1,916,000)
Puebla (836,000)
Léon (656,000)
Ciudad Juárez (567,000)
Culiacán (560,000)
Mexicali (511,000)
Tijuana (461,000)
Mérida (425,000)
Acapulco (409,000)
Chihuahua (407,000)
San Luis Potosí (407,000)

Language: Spanish is the official language. Indian languages are also spoken, including Maya, Mixtec, Náhuatl, Otomí and Zapotec.

Highest point: Orizaba (Citlaltépetl). an extinct, snow-capped volcano, southeast of Mexico City, 5,700 m (18,700 ft) above sea-level. It is North America's third highest peak.

Longest river: The Rio Bravo (Rio Grande in the US). The river's total length is 3,925 km (1,880 miles), of which about 2,100 km (1,305 miles) form part of Mexico's northeastern border with the US.

Largest lake: Lake Chapala, in the state of Jalisco, measures 86 km (53 miles) in length by 25 km (16 miles) at its widest.

△ **A land area comparison**
Mexico's 1,972,547 sq km (761,605 sq m) of territory make it a small country in comparison with the US, which has 9,370,000 sq km (3,600,000 sq m), or Australia with 7,650,000 sq km (2,470,000 sq m). But Mexico is far larger than many European countries. Britain, for example, has a land area of only 229,979 sq km (88,759 sq m) and is therefore eight times smaller than Mexico.

Australia 2 per sq km

USA 25 per sq km

Mexico 39 per sq km

UK 231 per sq km

Cities and towns
66%   **Country** 34%

△ **Where people live**
Cities and large towns account for
two-thirds of Mexico's population.
Both Baja California and Yucatán
are sparsely populated.

△ **A population density
comparison**
Mexico's population has increased
greatly in recent years. But world-
wide it is still rated as medium-
low. There is a very unequal
distribution between rural areas
and the crowded, ever-expanding
cities.

▷ **Major population centers**
Most people live on the Central
Plateau. The areas in and round
the larger ports also have
substantial populations.

Home life

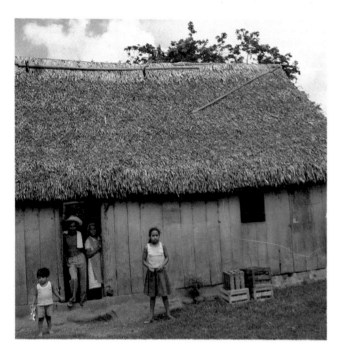

Above: A traditional house in a small village in central Mexico.

Below: A birthday provides the occasion for a family gathering near Veracruz.

The Mexican's home may be a modern urban apartment, a simple village dwelling, or a shanty on the edge of an industrial town. It may even be a mansion situated in an elegant quarter of Mexico City. Whatever its size or style, the house usually shelters a large and close-knit family.

In Mexico the average household has between six and ten members, and includes several generations. The grandparents share in the education of the young as much as the father and mother, and will be left to look after the house and children if both parents go out to work.

Grown-up, unmarried children – especially girls – almost always live at home. Girls continue to share in the running of the household even if they have an outside job. When they marry some may move in with their in-laws. Close contact is the main rule of family life in Mexico.

Left: A living room with simple and practical furniture. There is a radio and record player, but no television.

Below: This family, who live on the outskirts of Mexico City, are a typical example of the modern urban family.

It is almost always the women – either female members of the family, or a maid if there is one – who do the cooking and cleaning in a Mexican household. Cooking is usually elaborate, because mealtimes are regarded as important family occasions. For this reason the family home, however small, will generally have a proper dining room where old and young can sit down together. Bedrooms are nearly always shared, too, regardless of the social and economic standing of the family.

After the evening meal, the family will usually listen to the radio or gather round the television set if they have one. Throughout the year there are special celebrations to enjoy. Frequent national holidays herald parades and fireworks. Weddings and christenings bring gatherings of friends and relations which are followed by large, lavish parties. Mexicans love music and dancing, and spare no expense when a member of the family has reason to celebrate. Old or young, married or single, most Mexicans think, live and enjoy themselves as a family unit.

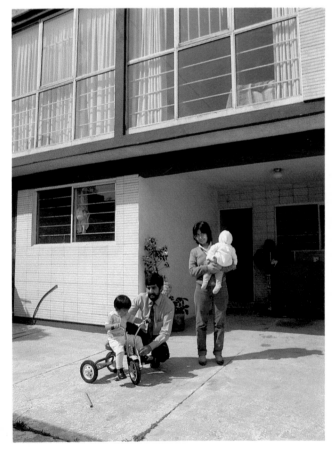

Shops and shopping

Most visitors to Mexico are immediately impressed by the vivid colours of goods on sale in the shops. Among the brightest are traditional blankets and shawls, hand-painted figurines, shiny red chilies and gleaming copperware.

In villages or rural areas trading often takes place at an outdoor market, or *tiangui*. The *tiangui* consists of a length of canvas on which the goods are laid, with a second piece hoisted above to make a roof. There are no fixed prices at *tianguis*, everyone haggles. The general bustle at outdoor markets is sometimes accompanied by lively music provided by local bands.

Most towns also have indoor markets housed in large, airy halls which were built at the beginning of the century or even earlier. Large numbers of street vendors can be seen in most cities. They sell almost anything from pet animals to toys and chinaware.

Above: In rural areas many people bring their goods to sell in open-air markets.

Below: Large indoor markets are common in every town and city. They sell a vast range of goods.

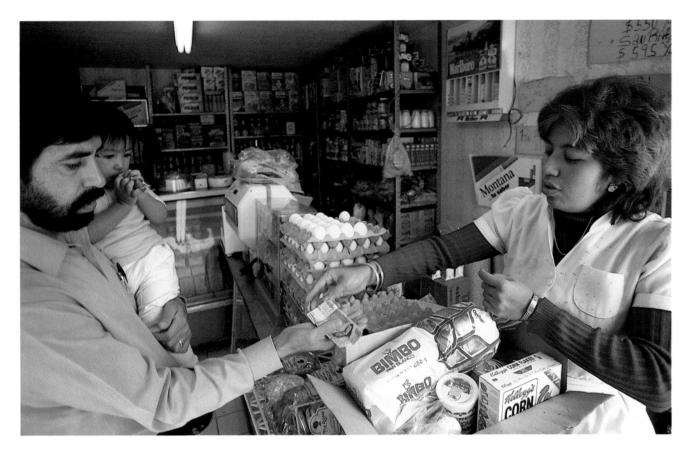

Small shops and stalls are found throughout Mexico. Handicraft dealers sell local pottery, silverwork and woven baskets, while the local grocery store will have shelves laden with food, especially herbs and spices.

Shopping in Mexico is often a social activity, as in many other countries. While shopping many people catch up on the local news and gossip. Local shops are open long hours and attract many people because of the personal attention given to customers. Supermarkets are also popular, especially with the more affluent families who are able to drive to the stores by car and so take advantage of cheaper bulk purchases.

Shopping in the large cities, such as Mexico City and Guadalajara, is often more impersonal, although the choice of goods is wider. As well as large markets, these cities have elegant boutiques and busy department stores which are open from 9.30 a.m. to 5.30 p.m. Their prices are too high for many people and they cater mostly for the affluent Mexican and the tourist trade.

Above: A local shop. Small grocers are very common and offer a wide range of foods.

Below: A shopping arcade in Guanajuato. It stocks modern merchandise and the latest fashions.

Cooking and eating

For Mexicans, meals are usually family occasions. Breakfast is always simple, consisting of coffee and bread or buns. Until recent times lunch was an elaborate meal. In small towns and in rural areas it is still the most important meal for most families. Dinner has, however, now become the main meal in large cities, where the distance between home and work may be considerable. The family can be together for a meal only in the evening.

Meals are usually accompanied by drinks such as fruit juices. Adults often have wine and beer, and sometimes the strong spirit known as *tequila*.

Mexico has given the world one of the most distinctive styles of cooking, and also a great many foodstuffs. Tomatoes, chocolate, vanilla and peanuts are just a few of the foods that originally came from Mexico and are now eaten throughout the world.

Above: The family have a modern kitchen. Most meals are eaten in a dining room.

Below: A family sits down to an outdoor meal. On the menu are chicken, *tortillas* and soft drinks.

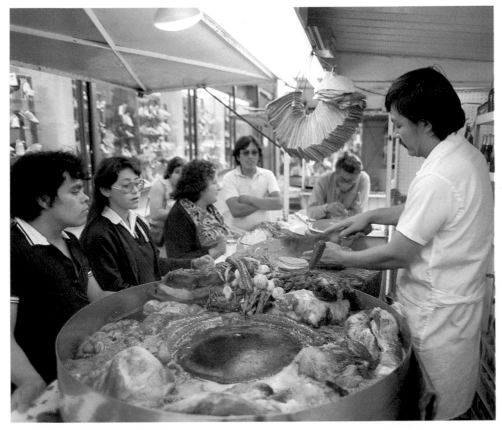

Left: A snack can be obtained quickly at a *tortilla* bar. A wide range of fillings are available.

Below: *Chili con carne* is made with meat, beans, chili peppers, onions and spices. It is one of Mexico's most famous dishes.

Corn is the country's most important basic food. Since ancient times it has been used to make flat pancakes called *tortillas*. They are eaten like bread or made into a snack called a *tacos* with different fillings. Beans are another important ingredient in the Mexican diet, either cooked and eaten on their own, or mixed with other ingredients. Beans are used in one of the most famous Mexican dishes – *chili con carne*.

Mexico has many other dishes that are not well known outside the country. One of these is *mole poblano.* It consists of chicken or turkey cooked in an elaborate sauce or *mole* made up of 30 to 40 ingredients including unsweetened chocolate, which gives the dish its brown color. Like many Mexican dishes, it is a blend of Indian and Spanish cooking.

Throughout Mexico *tortilla* and *taco* stands provide people with quick, freshly cooked meals at any time of the day. Most large towns and cities also have restaurants offering a variety of national and international dishes. These are popular and bustling places at lunchtime, when they are filled with workers and shoppers.

Pastimes and sports

Many of Mexico's pastimes and sports have their origins in Spain, but games from other countries, such as soccer, volleyball and tennis, are also popular.

Mexico played host to the world for the 1968 Olympic Games, and has been the venue for soccer's World Cup finals in 1970 and 1986. Soccer is the country's leading spectator sport. Matches held on local grounds or in huge stadiums such as the Azteca Stadium in Mexico City attract large, enthusiastic crowds. Other spectator sports with a large following include bullfighting introduced from Spain and baseball from the US. People also like the handball game known as *jai alai*, which originated in the Basque region of Spain.

Jogging is a popular activity, as in many countries, as a means to keep fit. For the less energetic, walking in the large city parks is a favourite pastime, often involving all the family.

Above: Most Mexicans are soccer enthusiasts. The national team, here playing England in 1983, has a devoted following.

Below: Bullfighting was introduced by the Spanish and is still popular, though soccer draws larger crowds.

Left: Mexican cowboys or *charros*, display their riding skill in rodeo-like *charreadas*.

Below: An Indian-style pageant before the church of Our Lady of Guadalupe in Mexico City.

Mexicans take fiestas and festivals very seriously, and celebrate them in style. Their national holidays include Christmas, Independence Day and Labor Day, but many other events, such as those marking Mexico's progress to democracy, are also celebrated. Most towns and villages also have their own local fiestas – usually in honor of their patron saint.

Christmas celebrations are extremely elaborate. On of the highlights for the children is the breaking up of the *piñata*. This is the name given to a brightly painted bag full of toys which is hung from the ceiling. The children are given poles which they use to break open the bag – hoping to bring down the shower of gifts.

At holiday time, many Mexican families like to attend *charreadas*. At these typical Mexican events, horsemen display riding, lassoing and other skills. The *charreadas* derive their name from the traditional costume of the riders, which is similar to that still worn by villagers of the province of Salamanca in Spain at their various fiestas.

News and broadcasting

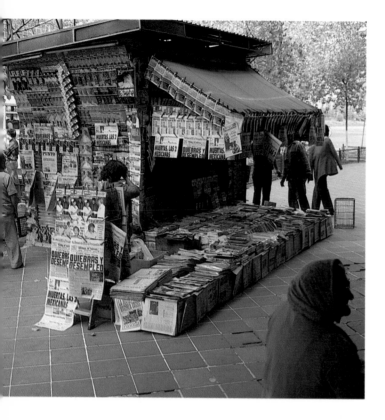

Mexico has 380 newspapers, representing all shades of political opinion. The press enjoys great freedom of expression and debates national and international issues in a lively and forthright manner.

Altogether, the newspapers produce a total of nine million copies, putting the country in 13th place in the world in terms of circulation. Mexico City alone has 17 daily papers which print, between them, just under two million copies. Many of the papers have a great number of pages – *Novedades*, for example, may have 90 pages.

Other means of mass communication have also expanded greatly. The country now has, for example, 1,061 stations broadcasting radio programs, of which about a thousand are commercial. The total number of radios is approximately 20.5 million, and Mexico has, per person, one of the highest concentration of radios in the world.

Above: Mexicans are avid newspaper readers and have a free and open press.

Right: A huge range of publications are available, both produced in Mexico and imported. Among the most popular are fashion and sports magazines.

Left: Mexican Television (Televisa) filming an Indian festival in Mexico City.

Below: Jacobo Zabludousky, a popular television presenter.

Bottom: Lucia Mendez, a Mexican television star.

Ownership of television sets is low compared with some countries, as only 68 per cent of households have sets. Almost a third of these are in Mexico City. The national network, Televisa, has its studios in Mexico City. Throughout the country there are 211 television stations, of which eight are devoted exclusively to educational and cultural broadcasts. It is also possible to watch programs beamed directly from countries such as the United States.

Book publishing is a very dynamic sector of Mexico's communication industry. The first printing press in the New World was used in Mexico City in 1539, and books have been an important aspect of Mexican culture ever since. Until the 1930s Spanish publishers exported books to Latin America in large numbers. The Spanish Civil War interrupted this trade. Mexico stepped in to fill the gap and it has since then remained a leader in the field. At present, some 5,000 titles are published in Mexico each year. Most are in Spanish and go to markets on both sides of the Atlantic.

Fact file: home life and leisure

Key facts

Population composition: People under 15 years of age make up 46.2 per cent of the population; people between 15 and 64 make up 50.5 per cent; and people over 65 make up 3.3 per cent.

Average life expectancy: 66 years (1983), as compared with 55 years in 1960. (By comparison, people in the US live, on average, 75 years, while people in India live only 55 years.) Women make up 50.6 per cent of the population. On average, women live to an age of 68 years, four years more than men.

Rate of population increase: Between 1960 and 1970 the population of Mexico increased at the high rate of 3.3 per cent per year. Between 1973 and 1982 it was at 2.9 per cent per year. An average rate of 2.3 per cent per year is forecast for the period 1980–2000.

Family life: The average age when men marry is 20–25 years; many women marry before they are 20. The average size of households is about eight. The length of holidays depend on the time at work, but a minimum of six days is granted after one year's service.

Work: In 1982 the average workweek was 40.2 hours in Mexico. The workforce in 1980 was 22,066,084. Unemployment in 1986 had risen to 25 per cent, largely as a result of the fall in world oil prices.

Prices: Prices rose by 3.5 per cent a year in 1960–70, and by 20.9 per cent in 1970–82. High inflation and the drop in world oil prices caused the peso to be devalued by 40 per cent in 1982.

Religions: In 1980, Roman Catholics made up 92.6 per cent of the population, Protestants 3.3 per cent, and people of other religions 4.1 per cent.

Vacuum cleaner	6%
Refrigerator	13%
Telephone	23%
Car	25%
Washing Machine	36%
Television	68%

Other goods and services	5%
Clothing and shoes	8%
Vehicles	11%
Education and Amusement	15%
Housing	17%
Food	44%

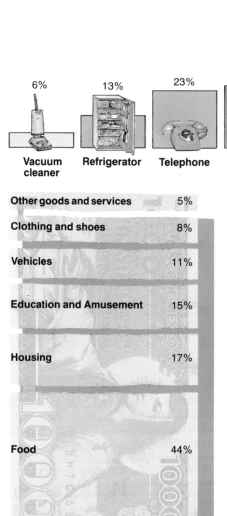

△ **How many households owned goods in 1984**
The ownership of television sets and other consumer durables, are low in comparison with the US and European countries. There has been a surge in ownership of such goods in recent years.

◁ **How the average household budget was spent in 1984**
Rents in Mexico are quite low. Education and entertainment are an increasing part of family expenditure.

▽ **Mexican stamps and money**
The *peso* is divided into 100 *centavos*. Banknotes come in denominations of 100, 500, 1,000, 2,000, 5,000 and 10,000 *pesos*. There are coins of 1, 5, 10 and 50 *pesos* and also coins of 20 and 50 *centavos*.

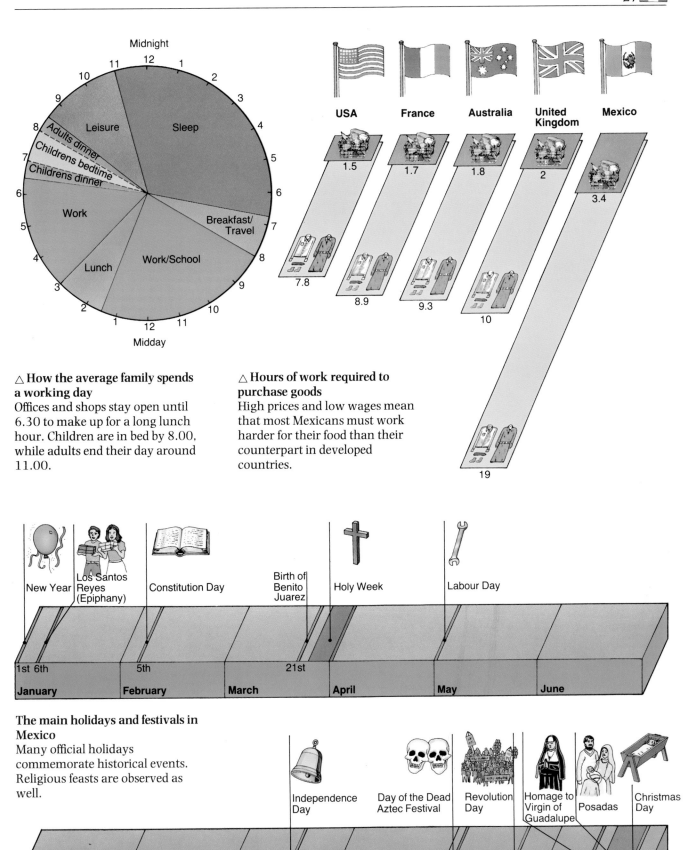

USA   **France**   **Australia**   **United Kingdom**   **Mexico**

△ **How the average family spends a working day**

Offices and shops stay open until 6.30 to make up for a long lunch hour. Children are in bed by 8.00, while adults end their day around 11.00.

△ **Hours of work required to purchase goods**

High prices and low wages mean that most Mexicans must work harder for their food than their counterpart in developed countries.

The main holidays and festivals in Mexico

Many official holidays commemorate historical events. Religious feasts are observed as well.

Farming and fishing

Only about half of Mexico is suitable for agriculture because of Mexico's dry climate and rugged mountainous terrain. In some parts of the country artificial irrigation is needed throughout the year.

Until the 19th century, most of Mexico was in the hands of a few powerful landowners. Since then there have been laws and reforms to redistribute the land, some of it is farmed under the *ejido* system. Under this system the government owns the land, but allocates certain areas to people who work it and then keep the profits. Farmers grow both food crops (which are used to feed themselves), and cash crops which are sold in the markets and also exported.

The main commercial farming areas are in irrigated parts of the north of the country, where cotton and wheat are the chief crops. Fruit and vegetables, such as melons and tomatoes, are grown along the fertile river valleys.

Forests 25%

Grazing land 38%

Arable land 12%   Mountains and urban 25%

Above: Land use in Mexico. The scarce arable land, where necessary, is irrigated to make it yield more crops.

Below: Ox-drawn carts, unchanged for centuries, are still a common sight in many rural areas of Mexico.

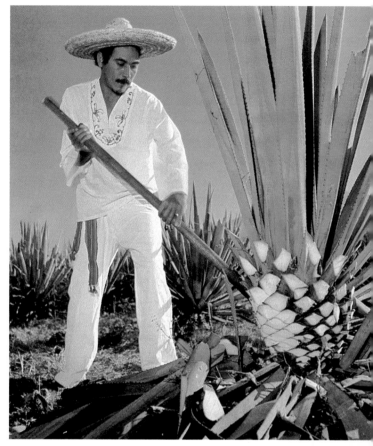

Above: Mexico grows a large amount of fruit. Apples, bananas and citrus fruits grow well along the river valleys.

Right: The blue agave plant is the source of the strong drink called *tequila*.

Below: Fishing nets on the Pacific Coast.

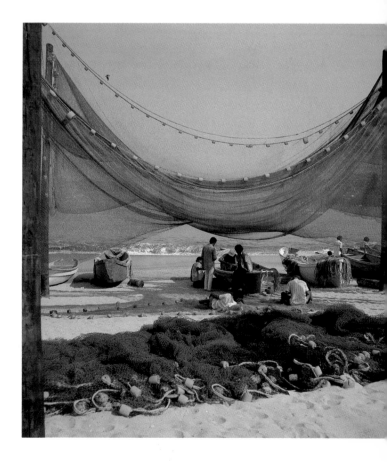

Mexico is the world's sixth largest meat producer. Cattle are reared in semi-arid areas of the north, and sheep are grazed on the Central Plateau. The most rugged areas are suitable only for goats.

Sugar cane, coffee, and fruit are important crops on the southern plains. Between 1976 and 1982, fruit production expanded by over 50 per cent. The main food crop, however, is corn, which is grown on nearly half the cultivated land. Even so, Mexico still has to import corn to satisfy demand.

With the introduction of refrigerated trucks, fishing has developed into a major industry. It provides employment not only for fishermen, but also for retailers and distributors who handle the catches of tuna, sardines, anchovies, squid and a variety of shellfish. The most important catches are of shrimp, many thousand tons of which are exported.

Forestry is becoming increasingly important. Most of the timber, which includes both hard and soft woods, is used for lumber.

Natural resources

Mexico's greatest asset has always been its mineral wealth. The Spanish swiftly developed the rich silver deposits of Mexico. In recent times the discovery and exploitation of oil and gas has helped the growth of Mexican industry.

Mexico was already one of the world's major oil producers in 1922, but it was the huge new reserves discovered along the gulf coast and offshore in 1976 that provided the revenues for the beginning of an industrial boom. By 1983 the country was producing 2.3 million barrels of oil a day, about one-twentieth of world production. Mexico is now the world's fourth largest oil producer, and the fifth largest in the production of natural gas.

The many rivers which cascade down the steep valleys of the Central Plateau provide Mexico with vast amounts of hydroelectric power. Today over one-third of Mexico's energy requirements are provided by hydroelectric schemes.

Below: A large hydro-electric dam at Villahermosa. More than a third of Mexico's electricity is generated by hydro-electric plants.

Above: Oil production in Mexico is government controlled by PEMEX (Petroleos Mexicanos). Its revenues are vital to Mexico's economy.

Mexico is also endowed with a great many precious metals and other minerals that are vital to industry. The country leads the world in silver production, is second in the production of graphite and bismuth, third in mercury production, and fourth in arsenic and selenium.

Other important minerals include sulphur, lead, zinc, coal, uranium, iron ore, gold and copper. Minerals represent the fourth largest source of export revenue for Mexico after oil, agricultural products and machinery.

Mining employs over 160,000 people directly, with another 1.6 million people involved in related industries.

Some of the minerals, such as coal, provide primary sources of energy while others are used to make vital components in manufacturing. The country's large cement industry gets its raw materials, sand, gravel and crushed stone, from local quarries. Mexico's large craft industry draws on the nation's vast deposits of precious metals, especially silver.

Above left: Mexico's main steel works are located at Monterrey and Monclova, close to the Sabinas coalfields.

Above: One of the richest silver mines in Mexico near Guanajuato.
Below: Tapping for resin is a profitable industry.

Industry and trade

Mexico's economy flourished during the oil boom of the 1970s, creating many new jobs. A fall in world oil prices in the 1980s slowed the expansion considerably, but much of the nation's industry is now sufficiently modernized to compete in world markets.

Most of Mexico's industry is located around Mexico City, Guadalajara, Orizaba and Puebla. Farther north, extensive coalfields fuel the iron and steel plants at the nearby cities of Monterrey and Monclova.

Oil, gas and products from the petrochemical industry are the chief sources of overseas currency, and represent nearly 80 per cent of all exports. Mexico's main trading partners are the United States and Japan, Europe and Latin America.

Increased car ownership has been one of the most visible signs of the country's economic progress. Today, demand for cars exceeds production. There are seven assembly plants in the country, which in 1980 produced 430,000 vehicles.

Above: Car manufacture and assembly is an increasingly important industry. Here, a Chevrolet is ready to leave the assembly line.

Left: Food processing accounts for one quarter of Mexico's industrial production, and employs half a million people. This plant is producing *tequila*.

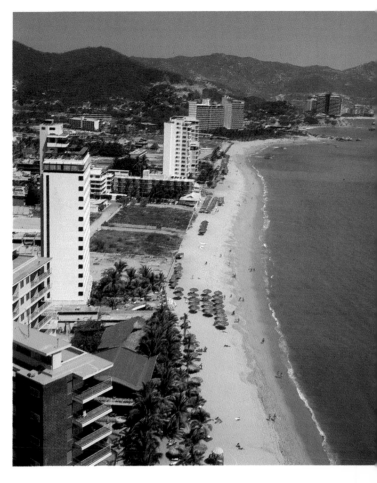

Tourism is the second largest source of currency in Mexico. The country's rich and colorful heritage, as well as its breathtaking scenery and extensive beaches, attracted 4,749,000 visitors in 1983. One of the most famous resorts is Acapulco on the western Pacific coast, although the Caribbean coast boasts equally fine beaches with the added attractions of the Yucatán Peninsula and its Mayan ruins.

Food processing, electronics and the production of office equipment, are all part of Mexico's light industry, These and other activities are closely related to the tourist industry, They include glassware, textiles, woollen goods and handicrafts. Products based on traditional designs range from gold and silver jewelry to basketware.

Other important industries in Mexico include the construction industry, which employs seven per cent of the working population, and the manufacture of timber products.

Above left: Typewriters being assembled at a large IBM factory in Mexico City.

Above: A tourist resort.
Below: Traditional designs are popular with tourists.

Transportation

Mexico has a modern and extensive system of highways despite the mountainous nature of the country. There are more than 42,000 km (26,100 miles) of proper paved macadam roads, many of which converge on Mexico City and provincial capitals, such as Guadalajara. Routes radiating from Mexico City connect the capital with other major towns and ports. Running the length of the country is the Pan American Highway, a highway system linking the United States with 17 Latin American countries.

In 1983 the total number of motor vehicles in Mexico exceeded seven million, of which 67 per cent were cars and 24.5 per cent were trucks. About two-fifths of the nation's motor vehicles are found in Mexico city.

In the cities buses are inexpensive and run frequently. Buses are a popular means of transport and come in all shapes and sizes from luxury coaches with air conditioning which are used for long journeys and old, rattling vehicles which serve the isolated rural districts.

Above: This ferry or *panga* crosses the Grijalva River in the southern state of Tabasco. It provides an essential link for many people.

Below: A shared taxi and a bus on a highway out of Mexico City. Both are popular and inexpensive forms of transport in Mexico.

Above: An airliner from Aero-mexico's fleet at Villahermosa, in the southern part of the Gulf of Mexico.

Right: Mexico has 23,300 km (14,500 miles) of railroad which has to traverse very often difficult terrain.

Air transport has expanded greatly in recent years. By 1984 some 18 million passengers passed through Mexico's airports during the course of a year.

The main shipping ports are at Veracruz, Tampico, Coatzalcoacos, Salina Cruz, Manzanillo, Acapulco and Lázaro Cardenas. Veracruz, on the Gulf of Mexico, is the leading port. Located close by are the installations of Pajaritos, which handle most of the shipments for the petroleum industry.

The railroads are government-run apart from three small lines in private hands. The state railroads receive a subsidy which makes the fares cheap and the cargo rates especially low. For this reason more cargo is moved by rail in Mexico than in many other more industrialized countries. Mexico City also has a subway system, decorated in Indian, Mexican and Spanish styles. It is as crowded during rush hours as any similar system elsewhere.

Fact file: economy and trade

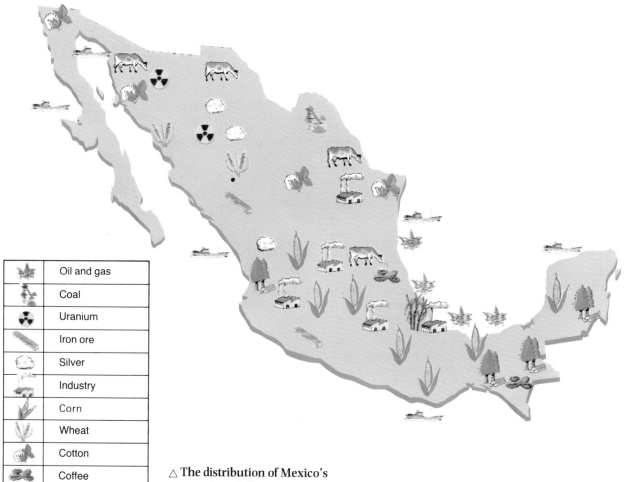

	Oil and gas
	Coal
	Uranium
	Iron ore
	Silver
	Industry
	Corn
	Wheat
	Cotton
	Coffee
	Sugar cane
	Cattle
	Fishing port
	Forestry

△ **The distribution of Mexico's economic activity**
Corn, the most important crop, is grown in central and southern regions. The main industrial zones are on the Central Plateau while the largest silver mines are in the north.

Key facts

Structure of production: Of the total GDP (the value of all economic activity in Mexico), farming, forestry and fishing contribute 7 per cent, industry 38 per cent, and services (such as commerce and the civil service) 55 per cent.
Farming: Crops are grown on about 12 per cent of Mexico's land area. Grazing land makes up another 38 per cent. *Main products:* cotton, coffee, fruit, wheat, sorghum, corn.

sugar cane, vegetables.
Mining: In the early 1980s, Mexico became the second largest oil producer in the Americas, overtaking Venezuela. Other minerals include silver, coal, iron, copper, gold, lead, sulphur, manganese, tin, uranium and zinc.
Manufacturing: Mexico has expanded its manufacturing industries greatly in the last 40 years. Major products now include chemicals, machinery, clothing, processed foods, processed

petroleum and steel.

Trade (1983): Total imports: US $7,720 million; exports: US $21,398 million. Mexico is the fourth most important trading Nation in the Americas, after the US, Canada and Brazil.
Economic growth: The average growth rate of Mexico's gross national product between 1973–82 was 6.2 per cent a year. This high rate reflected the rapid development of the oil industry.

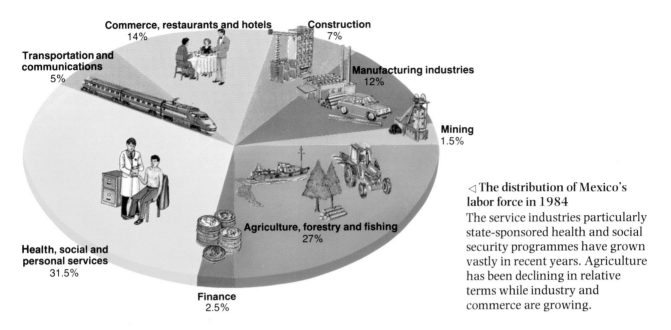

Commerce, restaurants and hotels
14%

Construction
7%

Transportation and communications
5%

Manufacturing industries
12%

Mining
1.5%

Health, social and personal services
31.5%

Agriculture, forestry and fishing
27%

Finance
2.5%

◁ The distribution of Mexico's labor force in 1984
The service industries particularly state-sponsored health and social security programmes have grown vastly in recent years. Agriculture has been declining in relative terms while industry and commerce are growing.

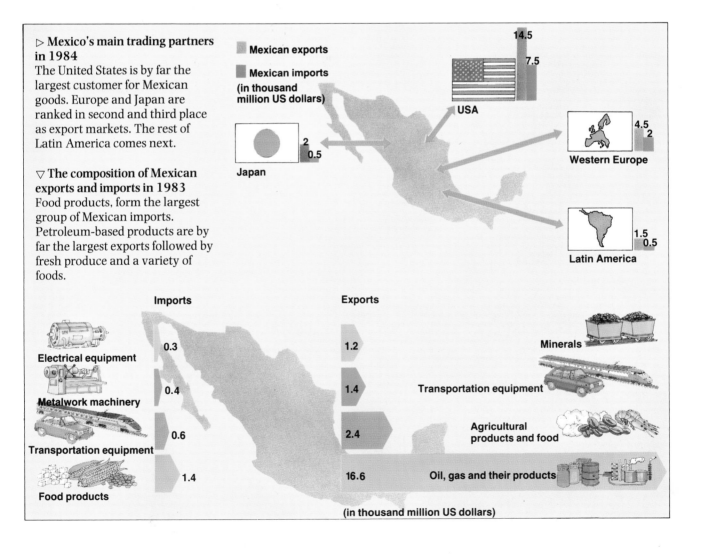

▷ Mexico's main trading partners in 1984
The United States is by far the largest customer for Mexican goods. Europe and Japan are ranked in second and third place as export markets. The rest of Latin America comes next.

▽ The composition of Mexican exports and imports in 1983
Food products, form the largest group of Mexican imports. Petroleum-based products are by far the largest exports followed by fresh produce and a variety of foods.

Mexican exports

Mexican imports
(in thousand million US dollars)

USA
14.5
7.5

Japan
2
0.5

Western Europe
4.5
2

Latin America
1.5
0.5

Imports

Exports

Electrical equipment
0.3

1.2
Minerals

Metalwork machinery
0.4

1.4
Transportation equipment

Transportation equipment
0.6

2.4
Agricultural products and food

Food products
1.4

16.6
Oil, gas and their products

(in thousand million US dollars)

Education

Few developing countries have expanded education as vigorously as Mexico. After the 1910 Revolution, hundreds of schools were opened throughout the country. The fight for literacy gradually brought results, with a great leap forward between 1960 and 1980. By 1983, the number of people who could read and write had risen to 90 per cent.

In Mexico education is compulsory and free between the ages of six and 16. Before the age of six, some Mexican children attend a pre-school course for two years. Primary (elementary) education lasts six years and is divided into two levels, basic and higher, each taking three years. Secondary education consists of a three-year basic curriculum, and a further three years for pupils intending to go to university.

Primary school children begin their day at 8 in the morning and finish at 1.00 p.m. Modern teaching methods are used in Mexican schools, but discipline is strict and the teacher still a figure of respect.

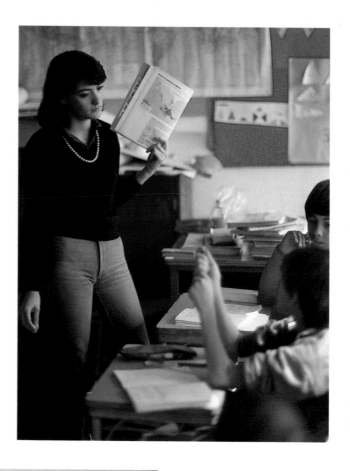

Above: A primary school. Education at Mexican primary schools is free and compulsory from the age of six.

Left: The government has allocated large sums of money to build new schools and supply educational equipment for the growing population of Mexicans.

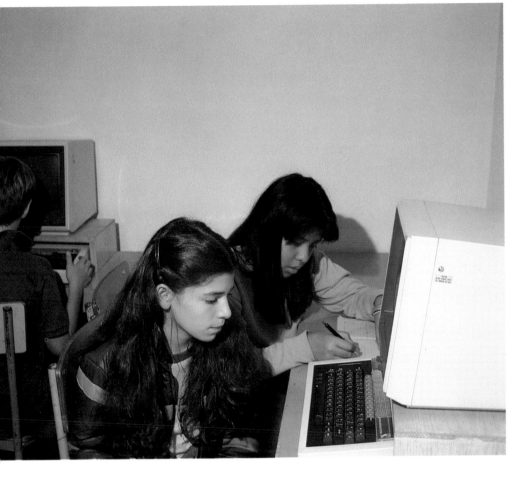

Left: Pupils using the school's computers. Many classrooms have this type of modern equipment.

Below: Students at the National University of Mexico City. A vast mosaic decorates the main library building.

Since education in Mexico is now compulsory, nearly all children are registered at a school. Mexico has achieved enrollment figures of 98 per cent for children of primary school age, and 88 per cent for children of secondary level. Even remote areas can now receive educational broadcasts by means of Mexico's recently launched communications satellite.

Most schools in Mexico are government run. There are also many church schools which are not supported by the government. They make, however, a very valuable contribution to the educational system, especially at the secondary-school level.

For the student who goes on to higher education there are more than 300 professional schools, including state universities, teacher-training schools and technical colleges. In 1984 over a million students were pursuing higher education. The country's oldest and largest university is in Mexico City.

The arts

The many great Indian civilizations have provided Mexico with a vast cultural treasures, including beautiful temples and impressive sculptures. Folk arts derived from ancient Indian cultures still survive. The ceramic, weaving and silverwork crafts are particularly distinguished.

But art is by no means a thing of the past in Mexico. In the early 20th century, a number of Mexican artists achieved lasting fame for their new approach to mural painting. These included José Clemente Orozco (1883–1949), David Siqueiros (1898–1974), Diego Rivera (1886–1957), and Rufino Tamayo (1899–).

Among the country's most noted composers is Carlos Chávez (1899–1978,) whose symphonic and chamber music has become part of the modern repertoire in both America and Europe. In 1952 the Mexican dancer Amalia Hernández formed the Ballet Folklórico. This dance group has two companies touring the world, and a third at the Palace of Fine Arts in Mexico City.

Above: A Mayan sculpture. Mexico's Indian heritage is the inspiration of many of its 20th century artists.

Below: *The Time Machine* is one of Diego Rivera's colourful murals which depict social and political themes in world history.

Left: Sor Juana Inés de la Cruz, the brilliant and outspoken writer. Her prose and poetry rank among the finest of the 17th century.

Above: Octavio Paz, poet, critic and interpreter of the Mexican character.

Below: The entrance to Mexico City's Satellite Town.

But it is in literature that Mexico has, perhaps, made the greatest contribution to world culture. A long line of poets, dramatists, political writers and novelists have enriched the literature of both Spain and the New World. Among them is a 17th-century nun Sor (Sister) Juana Inés de la Cruz (1651–95), whose poetry ranks with the finest in the Spanish language. Her interest in politics and her scientific mind made her a remarkable person, far ahead of her time.

Mexico has also produced such modern writers as Juan Rulfo (1918–86), Carlos Fuentes (1928–) and Octavio Paz (1914–). Rulfo, was the founder of the "magical realism" school of fiction, while Fuentes remains at the forefront of Latin American novelists. The leading writer in contemporary Mexico is the poet and essayist Octavio Paz, whose works, like those of Fuentes, have been translated into most Western languages. His writings shed great light on the Mexican personality.

The making of modern Mexico

Mexico gained independence from Spain in 1821. The new government, however, could do little to improve conditions for the common people, because the rich, landed classes still effectively ruled the country.

In 1836, north of the Rio Grande, settlers from the United States revolted against Mexican rule, and proclaimed the Republic of Texas. General López de Santa Anna rode north to the settlers' fort – an old mission called "The Poplar" (El Alamo) – and killed most of the defenders. One month later the United States army attacked and defeated the Mexican army.

In 1846 American forces stormed Mexico City. Peace came when Santa Anna, then president, ceded Texas – and later California, New Mexico and parts of Arizona – to the United States. Benito Juárez, Minister of Justice, then ordered all church and army property seized and given to the needy. Conservative groups fought these measures and a bitter civil war ensued.

Above: General López de Santa Anna, President of Mexico during the war with the United States in 1846–7.

Left: The Alamo

Below: The land acquired by the United States from Mexico during and after the Mexican War. Mexico lost half of its land area.

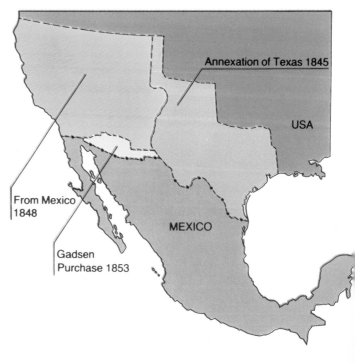

Annexation of Texas 1845

USA

From Mexico 1848

Gadsen Purchase 1853

MEXICO

Above: Archduke Maximilian of Austria is executed by firing squad in 1867. He was emperor of Mexico for only three years.

Right: Porfirio Díaz was President of Mexico for more than 30 years.
Below right: Peasants in revolt against the Díaz regime in 1910.

The war brought ruin to the economy and Juárez decided to delay payment of money owed to Spain, Britain and France. Soon all three countries landed troops to press their claims, but only the French chose to fight. Defeated initially at the Battle of Puebla (1862), France eventually routed Juárez.

In 1864 Mexican exiles, restored to power by the French, installed Archduke Maximilian of Austria as emperor. It was a short reign. Maximilian was captured in battle by Juárist forces in 1867, and promptly shot.

Under Porfirio Díaz's presidency (1876–1910), foreign investment grew. A thriving middle class also emerged, though peasants and workers still lacked the most basic human rights.

The sufferings of the poor exploded in the Mexican Revolution of 1910. It continued until the early 1930s, when socialist values became national policy. The Revolutionary Party, founded in 1929, assumed power that year and has remained in office ever since.

Mexico in the modern world

The oil boom begun in the 1970s brought enormous benefits to Mexico. It also posed a great problem – how to pay back the vast sums of money borrowed from other countries to develop a modern oil industry.

Despite the enormous strides made by Mexico, it became clear that the income produced by petroleum was not sufficient to meet repayments of the debt. Worse still, a drop in the price of oil in the 1980s meant the country's revenues were reduced.

In 1986 the Mexican government sought to obtain new terms for repayments of the debt. It also fought an economic recession, a 25 per cent unemployment rate and an annual inflation rate of 60 per cent. How well it copes with these problems will determine the future of the nation. If the government succeeds in reducing inflation and maintaining economic growth, there will be no loss of the benefits brought by the boom, and some hope of renewed growth in the future.

Above: The old and new in Mexico City. Sub-standard houses contrast sharply with modern high-rise buildings.

Left: Soccer fans at a match, during the World Cup, held in Mexico in 1986. Mexico has hosted several major events in recent years, including the Olympic Games.

Left: Rodolfo Neri, the first Mexican astronaut, went on a Space Shuttle mission in 1985. He was a crew member on a flight of the *Atlantis* shuttle.

Above: President Miguel de la Madrid Hurtado.
Below: Mexico has a vast young population. In 1983 43% of the people were under 14.

Relations between Mexico and the United States have become strained over the problem of migration. For decades, Mexicans have crossed the Rio Grande by the thousands in search of work. Lacking papers, few find new jobs, while virtually all are subject to arrest and even detention for illegally entering the United States.

To the south, Mexico is witnessing the unrest in El Salvador, Honduras, Guatemala and Nicaragua. As the leading voice of the Contadora Group – a regional alliance that includes Venezuela, Panama and Colombia – the Mexican government is pressing for a diplomatic solution to the crisis in Central America, a dangerous powder keg on its doorstep.

Its role in this and other regional problems is a significant one. Mexico is seen by other Latin American countries as an experienced negotiator with the United States, and is a leading spokesman for the nations that share its Spanish and Latin American traditions.

Fact file: government and world role

Key facts

Official name: *Estados Unidos Mexicanos* (United Mexican States)

National flag: Three vertical stripes of green, white and red. The central white stripe bears the coat of arms, which depicts an eagle on a cactus holding a snake.

National anthem: *Mexicanos, al grito de guerra.* (Mexicans, when you hear the war cry.)

National government: Mexico is a democratic federal republic. *Head of State:* The president, who is directly elected to a single, six-year term. The president heads the government and appoints the council of ministers and senior military and civilian officers of the state. *Congress:* The General Congress, the law-making parliament, consists of a 64-member Senate and a 400-member Chamber of Deputies. Senators serve six-year terms and deputies three-year terms.

Local government: The 31 states each have an elected governor and a Chamber of Deputies. The Federal District (Mexico City) is administered by a governor appointed by the president. The states are divided into local government areas, each with elected presidents and councils.

Defence: Enlistment into the regular army is voluntary, but for men aged 18 there is conscription into a part-time militia. *Army:* In 1985, the Army had a strength of 95,000. *Air Force:* The strength of the Air Force is about 5,500. *Navy:* In 1985, the Navy had 23,650 personnel.

Economic alliances: Mexico is a member of the Latin American Integration Association (LAIA), which took over from the Latin American Free Trade Association (LAFTA) in 1981.

Political alliances: Mexico is a member of the United Nations and of the OAS (Organization of American States), which is a regional organization of the United Nations. It is also a leading member of the Contadora Group (Mexico, Venezuela, Panama and Colombia).

△ **Mexico in the Americas**
Mexico forms part of the Organization of American States which has its headquarters in Washington. It is also a member of the United Nations. The Latin American Integration Association (LAIA), fosters trade among the states south of the Rio Grande.